# BREAKERS DOZEN

RAISED AND GLAZED COZY MYSTERIES,
BOOK 28

EMMA AINSLEY

SUMMER PRESCOTT BOOKS PUBLISHING

# CHAPTER ONE

Maggie Sharpe rolled over in her comfortable bed and pulled the blankets over her head. She was confused about the origin of the sharp pounding noises reverberating inside her bedroom. She rolled over and pulled the covers back from her head. Panic immediately set in when the morning sun shining through the bedroom window registered in her mind.

She was down the hall at her bathroom door before it dawned on her that she was not late for work. The moment she saw the yellow hard hat of the construction workers down the hall where the linen closet had been, she remembered the big home improvement project that had been going on for the past two weeks.

Maggie stared at the broad, sweaty back of the foreman, willing him not to turn around and see her in her night shirt. She quickly returned to her bedroom and shut the door behind her.

Her phone began to ring, and she raced to the table, pulling it off the charger.

"Were you sleeping?" Brett Mission asked her. Maggie smiled immediately. She was happy to hear from her fiancé every morning, and the closer their wedding date came, the more she considered how it would be to wake up next to him every morning for the rest of her life.

"I was walking down the hall trying to remember why there was so much racket," Maggie admitted with a chuckle. "I must have been in a really deep sleep."

"And you probably had a panic attack because you forgot that Naomi forced you to take a day off," Brett said.

"Guilty as charged, Sheriff," Maggie said.

"Do I know you, or do I know you?" Brett said. "What are you up to now?"

"I think I'm going to get dressed and figure out some coffee," she said. "I seem to remember the construction guys were going to have to turn off the water this morning, so I may have to take it to go from the donut shop."

"You know what's going to happen if you show up there on your day off?" Brett warned her.

"Oh, I know," Maggie said. "They'll try chasing me out of the place, but coffee is life, and I must do what I have to do."

"You're too funny," Brett said before he ended the phone call, promising to talk to her soon.

Maggie dressed and readied herself quickly. She slipped her boots on and grabbed an overcoat from a hook by the back door. She made it to her car without having to interact with any of the construction crew. It wasn't that she disliked them or even wanted to avoid interactions as a rule, but she knew there would be apologies all around if they realized she had been home the entire time.

Maggie started her car and backed out of the driveway without letting it warm up, despite the late November chill in the air. The donut shop was less than a block from her home, so warming the car up was never something she worried much about. Instead of parking in the alley behind the donut shop like normal, Maggie pulled around into the parking lot and entered through the front door like any other customer.

"What in the heck do you think you're doing?" Orson Hawley asked her from his seat at the Old Timer's table.

"I'm just here for coffee," Maggie said. She put her hands up in the air in surrender. "The crew has the water shut off this morning."

"Okay, then" Orson said, rising from his chair. "Do you want it black, or do you want a latte?"

"Orson, you go on and have your break," Maggie said. "I'll just order from Myra. I was going to grab a dozen for the crew anyway."

"I got it," Orson said, waving her off. "You go on, do whatever else you need to do, and I will take care of things. Now tell me what sort of coffee you want so I can get this together and you can get out of here."

Maggie shook her head and gave him her order for a cinnamon latte, a habit she had picked up from Brett. She headed to the restroom to wash her hands while Orson dashed behind the counter and began filling up a box from the display case. When she emerged, she was faced with three of her employees shaking their heads at her. Orson stood next to Myra Sawyer Macklin. Naomi Gardner wagged her finger at her.

"You're supposed to be anywhere but here," Naomi said.

"They have the water turned off at my house and I need coffee," Maggie said. She wanted to add that the constant pounding from the hammers during the demolition phase of the renovation had her on edge.

"Maybe you should take a drive somewhere," Ruby Cobb suggested. As Maggie's business partner and best friend, her words carried a little more weight than the others. She also understood how hard it was to take days off from work.

"I was thinking about driving out to Hunter Springs," Maggie said.

"Yes, going to visit the second location of your donut shop sounds exactly like taking a day off," Orson grumbled.

"Hey," Maggie said. "My grandson happens to be in Hunter Springs, too. Maybe I want to surprise him."

"Well, that's a little better," Orson said. Maggie was grateful she had finally met his approval on some level, even if she really planned to stop by the donut shop and visit with her son, Bradley.

"I'm going to run these donuts back by the house first," she said. "Thank you, guys. See you tomorrow." She picked up the large box and headed for the door.

In truth, Maggie was eager to talk over her plans

for a new donut variety with her son. She often prepared new varieties with Ruby in her large farmhouse kitchen or in the donut shop kitchen after work. Ruby's background as an executive chef with additional pastry chef training meant that she was often the one behind new menu additions. But once in a while, Maggie liked to be the one to create something new and shock her staff with the addition.

"See you in the morning," Orson called behind her. Maggie turned back and waved with her free hand.

Her car seemed even colder when she returned to it. She set the donut box on the passenger seat and drove back home. She pulled up in front of the house and left the car running while she removed the box of donuts and headed to the side of the house where three of the construction crew members stood.

"I brought breakfast," she said with a smile.

"Oh, thank you so much," the foreman said. His name was Jimmy, and he was barely a few years older than her own son. He was a hardworking professional. Maggie felt grateful that she had found him.

"I'm so happy you stopped by, and not just for the donuts. We have something we need to talk over with you."

"Okay," Maggie said. She immediately felt the

chill around her and shivered in her coat. Since the start of the house renovations, she had the worry of impending doom. Jimmy's words left her wondering if her worst home improvement disaster fears were about to come to fruition.

Jimmy waited while each of the other workers picked out a donut before he plucked one out of the box and set the rest of them on a tall step ladder. "I need you to follow me into the basement." He took a bite out of the donut and walked around the side of the house and through the back door. "We wanted to check out the foundation before we added weight with the new crawl space. So, I came down here with Tony, my foundation guy, and we found something a little weird." He pointed to the basement wall, the same wall she had seen many times over since inheriting the cottage house from her late aunt.

"I just see a concrete wall," Maggie said.

"And you are not wrong," Jimmy said. "But the weird part comes in when you notice how much newer the color of the wall appears compared to the floor and the other walls. And I don't know if you can tell, but the wall doesn't line up with the ceiling above it." Maggie looked up and shrugged her shoulders. She could easily see the lighter gray color of the concrete wall compared to the rest of the basement, but she was lost with the reference to the ceiling.

"I can't see it," she admitted.

Jimmy chuckled and shook his head. "It's tough to spot with an untrained eye," he said. "Look at the rafters on the end over here." He led her to the other side of the basement, and shone a flashlight on the rafters, following it down where the wood met the concrete wall.

"Okay," Maggie said.

"You can see where the wood beams end, right?" Maggie nodded her head. Jimmy walked back across the basement. "But when you take a look here, the ends of the rafters disappear in the concrete. Do you see the difference?"

Maggie nodded again and pointed to the rafters above her head. "Okay, yeah," she said. "I can see that."

"Do you have any idea what was done down here?" Jimmy asked. "Were you aware of any renovations on the basement?"

Maggie shook her head slowly. "Honestly, I have no idea," she said. "I inherited this property from my aunt a couple of years ago or so. Before that, she rented it out for a very long time."

"Okay," Jimmy said. "Well, my guess is that this

happened a little more than fifteen years ago. The house itself is about eighty years old and this is clearly new. But I also think there might be an older wall behind it."

"An older wall? Do you mean this wall was put here in front of the original wall?"

Jimmy nodded his head. "That's what I'm afraid of," he said.

"Why would anyone do this?" Maggie asked. She reached her hand out and brushed the wall. "It just doesn't make sense to me."

"That's the reason I wanted to have you come down here with me to look at this," Jimmy said. He pointed at the wall. "This is a red flag to me. There are a number of things that could have happened here, and not one of them makes me feel like we should move ahead with the renovation until we figure out what might be going on behind the wall."

"What do you mean by red flags?" Maggie asked.

"Well." Jimmy pushed his hat back on his head. "I'm worried this might have been installed to cover up a crumbling original wall or a bad water leak. This might have been a hasty, quick fix to cover up something that should have been fixed a long time ago. I don't want to get into the rest of the project and find out that this basement wall can't take the added weight."

Maggie sighed. She threw up her hands and shrugged her shoulders. "I suppose we have no choice," she said. "I would rather you find out what's going on before we have a bigger issue to deal with."

# CHAPTER TWO

Maggie drove toward Hunter Springs in a somber mood. She was consumed with dread and wondered if the construction crew would find something so terrible that the rest of the house would be doomed to demolition.

She was about ten minutes from the donut shop when she gave up and decided to call Brett. Under normal circumstances, she would not dream of calling him while he was at work unless it was an emergency. But she knew that he wouldn't answer if he was in the middle of anything too important, or dangerous.

"What's wrong, honey?" he said as soon as he answered the phone.

"It's the house," Maggie said with a sigh. "Jimmy took me down to the basement and showed me where he thinks a false wall was built. He's worried that the wall is there to cover up something horrible about the original wall."

"Something like what?"

"Maybe a bad foundation crack or a water leak," she said.

"What is he going to do?" Brett asked her.

"I gave him the go ahead to tear it out," she said. "I don't think we have any other choice."

"You were right to tell him to move forward with it, Maggie," he said. "But you know what? Even if he finds something down there that means extended repairs, we will get through it. I don't care if we have to live in a tent behind the donut shop, I'm going to marry you in a few months and where we live won't even matter."

Maggie laughed. "I have to have an air mattress, though," she said. "I don't think I'm made for the hard, concrete ground."

"Deal," Brett said and laughed. "It's going to be okay, sweetheart. I promise."

Maggie hung up the phone with a smile on her face. She pulled off of the highway and headed for the old downtown area. She pulled into the wide alley behind the old filling station where the Hunter Springs Donut Shop was located and breathed in a sigh of relief. Brett was right. If they found out that the entire house had to be leveled and rebuilt, they would make it through. Brett already had his own place out in the country and there were plenty of other homes for sale in the area. She loved the convenience of her small home's proximity to the donut shop and the memories that came with the small cottage her great-aunt, Marjorie Getz, had left to her, but it would not be the end of the world if she had to make other plans.

Immediately after she walked inside the donut shop through the back door, all of her thoughts and concerns about the house in Dogwood Mountain had fluttered away.

"I want to make a coffee cream donut," she announced to her son Bradley and his manager, Zeke Soren.

"I have a few recipes to get inspiration from, but I want this donut to really taste like a cup of coffee and sweet creamer."

"Do you have those recipes handy?" Zeke asked her. "Oh, and good morning to you, too, Maggie."

"Yes, good morning." She chuckled and handed over her tablet with the recipes already loaded.

"I found the basic recipe, but I want the cream and the donut to have a coffee flavor that is unmistakable," she said. "But I also don't want it to be over-powering."

"Is this a yeast donut or a quick donut?" Bradley asked her. He looked over his friend's shoulder and read through the first recipe.

"It's basically a brioche," Zeke said.

"What I'm thinking will work is cream cheese and a homemade sweet cream flavored with instant coffee," Maggie said. "A few drops of coffee flavoring and an extra dose of vanilla to the dough is all it will take."

Zeke nodded his head. "I agree. That seems like the best approach," he said. "I'm not a big fan of a few of these recipes that simply call for vanilla cream and hazelnut spread in the middle. Do you want to try your plan now?"

Maggie nodded her head and smiled. "I was hoping you boys were in an indulgent mood." She headed into the cooler to search for ingredients. Bradley cleared space for her near a countertop mixer and watched while she mixed several bricks of cream cheese, heavy whipping cream, vanilla paste, lemon juice, and powdered sugar in a large metal bowl. She inserted the flat beater attachment and watched while the ingredients formed into a creamy mixture. She added a few tablespoons of coffee granules and stopped, stood back, and added two more before she dipped a clean spoon into the bowl and sampled the filling. "Oh, that is good," she said. "But I think it needs a bit more coffee flavor."

Zeke swooped in with a clean spoon of his own and dipped it into the bowl. He nodded his head in agreement. "I think more vanilla, too."

Maggie measured the additional granules and vanilla paste into the bowl and turned the mixer on again. A moment later, she located another spoon and sampled it. "Perfection." This time Bradley joined in and tried it for himself.

"Oh, wow." His eyes were wide. "That's amazing. I definitely think the donut itself should not be overly sweet, though."

"Yeah, I agree with that," Zeke said. He disappeared into the large store room and returned with a container of flour. Maggie instructed him on the brioche dough. She handed over the eggs one at a time as he mixed them into the tall, floor mixer.

An hour later, Maggie removed the fresh brioche donuts from the deep fryer and set them on a cooling rack until she could safely handle them. She filled a half dozen, then rolled each one individually in powdered sugar.

"Shall we try one?" she asked, handing the platter of donuts over to her son.

"I say let's go for it," Zeke said. He swiped a donut from the platter and waited while the rest of them grabbed theirs. Maggie was the first to bite into the still-warm donut.

"Oh, Mom," Bradley said. "These are incredible."

Maggie helped herself to a second and a third bite. She was shocked at the deep coffee flavor and the sweetness.

"You're right on the money here, Maggie," Zeke said. "You've created a perfect balance of flavors."

"I think these taste like money," Bradley said with a mouth full of donuts. "Watch how fast these sell out."

"Let's give the rest out to your customers and see how it goes," Maggie suggested. She began pulling the donuts off of the cooling rack and filling them.

As she worked, her phone rang in her pocket. "Zeke, can you take over here?" she asked when she looked at the number on the screen. Her heart sank a little when she realized it was Jimmy's number. Zeke nodded and immediately took over from where she had left off. Maggie walked past the cooler to the back door and stepped outside.

"Hi, Jimmy," she said when she answered.

"Please don't tell me you found a secret floor on top of the old floor."

She expected the young man to chuckle, but the other end of the phone was silent until he cleared his throat.

"Maggie? Can you and the sheriff get over here?" he asked. His voice sounded hollow and distant. "I mean, now? We have a problem."

"Can you just tell me what the problem is over the phone, Jimmy?" Maggie asked. She was slightly annoyed that he hadn't led with that.

"Um, ma'am," he said, too formally. "You just need to get the sheriff and get over here as fast as you can. Please. This isn't something I'm comfortable telling you over the phone."

"Okay," Maggie muttered. "I'll be there in about a half hour." She ended the call and headed inside the donut shop kitchen.

"What's the matter?" Bradley asked when she came in. "You look like you've seen a ghost. Is Brett okay?"

Maggie nodded. "Something is going on with the renovation at the house, and I have to get over there as fast as I can," she said, not wanting to waste time explaining the issue with the basement wall. "I don't know exactly what the problem is, but my gut instinct tells me that it isn't good."

"Okay, well, call me as soon as you know something," Bradley said.

"Here, take these with you," Zeke said. He handed over a box of the brioche donuts and waved as she headed for the door.

Maggie drove a little over the speed limit all the way back to Dogwood Mountain. Her mind raced to answer why Jimmy asked for Brett to be there along with her, in the middle of the work day. She called Brett's cell phone, but it rang until the voicemail picked up. She shut the phone off without leaving a message and decided to wait until he called her. Surely, she could handle the problem on her own.

She found herself much more concerned than she thought possible when she pulled up to her house and found a driveway full of cars. The pickup truck Brett drove with the Dogwood Mountain Sheriff's Department decal on the doors was parked in the grass next to the garage.

"What's going on?" she called to Jimmy when she spotted him standing behind one of the cars she didn't recognize. He was engrossed in a stack of paperwork.

"Hold on a sec," he said to her, raising a finger. Maggie felt the hackles on the back of her neck raise.

She considered marching herself over to him and pulling him back by the collar of his safety vest and giving him a good talking to about respect and the proper way to do business but held back. Years of experience had told her that jumping to conclusions in such matters was often a direct path to embarrassment and making apologies she did not want to make.

"Ms. Sharpe." Jimmy looked up at last. "Can you join me over here for a moment?" Maggie walked around three cars and approached him with her arms folded.

"Can you please let me in on what's going on with my house?" she asked. Her tone was as light as she could make it.

"Yes, and I apologize for keeping you waiting," Jimmy said. His eyes were full of worry and something else she couldn't put a finger on. "This is the first time I've ever had to deal with anything like this." She noticed then that his hands were shaking.

"I still don't have any idea what we're dealing with here," Maggie said. "Who are all of these people?"

Her mind had run through some scenarios while she waited, but nothing that explained what she could see in front of her. If there was a gas leak, there would be fewer cars around her house, not more.

Brett appeared behind Jimmy. His face was tight with worry. "You can stay at my place until this gets resolved," he said grimly.

"Until what gets resolved?" Maggie shouted. "I still don't know what is going on around here!" She felt immediate embarrassment for her outburst.

"You haven't told her?" Brett asked Jimmy.

"No, the building inspector had me looking over something," Jimmy said. "But maybe it ought to come from you now, since you're standing right here."

"Will someone please tell me?" Maggie asked in a controlled voice.

Brett nodded and took her by the arm. He led her to the side of his truck and sighed. "While the crew was taking apart that wall downstairs, they found something. They had to stop what they were doing and call law enforcement immediately."

"What did they find?" Maggie asked. Her mind raced once again.

"Bones, Maggie," Brett said. "Specifically, a human hand. And they are pretty sure there's much more there. It appears that a wall was built in your basement to conceal a murder."

# CHAPTER THREE

Maggie sat on the tailgate of Brett's work truck. She was wrapped in a blanket Brett had brought her from the couch in the living room. Despite the cold temperatures outside, she couldn't bring herself to go inside the house while the police and the medical examiner stood around in the basement staring at the revelation behind the concrete wall.

"What are you going to do?" Brett asked her a little while later.

"I guess that depends on what you're going to do," Maggie admitted. "Am I going to end up a suspect in whatever happened downstairs?"

Brett laughed and wrapped his arms around her. "I don't think you have to worry about that," he said. "I already have a ballpark idea of how long that skeleton has been down there. And I have personal knowledge of when you moved into this house. You are not a suspect."

Maggie nodded her head. It might have been a silly thought, but she had the thought, nonetheless. She wasn't surprised to hear that Dr. Dana Marsh, the county coroner, was already on scene.

"I don't know what I am going to do," Maggie said. "I know I can go to your house, but that's awfully far from work. If I didn't have to be there so early, it probably wouldn't matter."

"Why don't you go and check in at the Dogwood House for a few days?" Brett said. "I bet Gretchen would love to put you up, and you will be close to work."

"I hate to ask this, knowing the gravity of the situation going on downstairs, but do you think this will be resolved in a few days? Is it practical to think this will all be wrapped up in a week?" Maggie asked. She felt so far out of her depth. "I know that's an awful question, but it's my house. It's different this time."

Brett leaned against the tailgate and shook his head. "It's not an awful question. It's fair that you want to know what's going to happen with your home and whether or not you're going to have to leave for a long time," he said. "As a matter of fact, I'm going to live here, too, and I want to know. Once the remains are removed, I'd count on another couple of days to collect evidence, and then that's all. Jimmy and his crew will repair what they can and then resume work on the house."

"Unless they find something else," Maggie added.

Brett nodded. "Unless they find something else," he said. "I think it would be safe to start with a week at the bed and breakfast."

"A week?" Maggie sighed. "One week isn't terrible, I guess." She slid off of the tailgate and nodded toward the house. "I'm going to have to go inside and get some things before I can leave. Is that even allowed?"

"I think if I go with you, there will be no questions asked," Brett said. "You think you can be in and out in fifteen minutes?"

"I can be in and out in five minutes," Maggie said.

"Let me go and inform Dr. Marsh about what's going on. Brooks is downstairs, too," Brett said. "I'm fairly sure he won't have an issue with you going inside the house." In addition to being married to Myra, Brooks Macklin was the local police chief. Maggie was grateful for their close relationship at that moment.

"I think I'll give Gretchen a call while you speak

with them, just to make sure she has a room available," she said. Brett headed around to the front of the house while Maggie walked back to her car to retrieve her cell phone.

Maggie called the number to the Dogwood House. She knew the number by heart. Since Gretchen had purchased the estate house that had also belonged to her Aunt Marjorie, the donut shop had made daily deliveries of pastries and coffee. She considered Gretchen a member of her extended family now, especially since she and Orson were something of a couple.

"Good morning, Maggie," Gretchen said when she picked up. "What can I do for you?"

"Rent a room to me for a few days," Maggie said. "Maybe a week."

"Why? What's going on?" Gretchen asked with genuine concern in her voice.

"The work crew ran into a problem in my house," Maggie said. "I have to be out of the house for at least few days while they resolve it." She planned to fill Gretchen in on everything later on, but for now she wanted to stick to the bare minimum of information.

"Sure," Gretchen said. "I can set you up with your own bed and bath. How does that sound?"

"Perfect," Maggie said, relieved.

"The question is, do you want your old childhood room, or would you prefer another one?" Gretchen asked.

"I don't mind either way," Maggie said. She was unsure if her old room would feel the same, but she did know that it was not connected to a bathroom.

"Okay, well, you just come on over whenever you're ready and I'll put you somewhere," Gretchen promised. "I've already heard that today is your day off."

"I wonder who could have told you that?" Maggie chuckled. It felt good to laugh at that moment. Without a doubt, she knew Orson had spilled the beans. He would likely do the same the next day when he delivered the donuts and coffee to the bed and breakfast. By then, news about the body in the basement will have gotten to everyone else.

Maggie hung up the phone just as Brett walked back around the garage.

"They're going to stop the excavation while we run inside," Brett said. He held up his hands and cocked his head to the side. "For the sake of the eventual investigation, I'm going inside with you just to close any loops that may come up as the investigation progresses. It's hard to believe there will be any evidence upstairs after all these years, but just in case."

"Does that mean I'm a potential suspect after all?" Maggie asked, still not convinced.

"No, no," Brett said. "It just means we're covering our bases as we move forward. That's all."

"Okay," Maggie said. She walked toward the house with Brett beside her. While she walked, she focused on making a mental list of what she needed to pack to take with her.

Brett waited, giving her space, while Maggie filled her suitcase with clothing for the week. She packed her toiletries and grabbed her laptop and a few more things before she declared she was finished.

"That was fast," Brett said.

"One more thing," Maggie said. She opened the cabinet next to the fridge and plucked a set of keys from the hook inside.

"What are those for?"

"An extra set of keys for the house," Maggie said, handing the keys over to him. "I should have given these to you the moment we got engaged. Anyway, while this investigation is going on, you should have them."

Brett nodded his head. "I wish there was a happier occasion for this moment but thank you."

Maggie left him with the keys and headed across town to the Dogwood House. She planned to call Ruby and fill her in on what was going on but decided that it could wait until she had settled in at the bed and breakfast.

Whatever she did, she planned to remain busy. Her mind raced to make sense of what was going on in her house. She just couldn't focus on the fact that a dead person had been below where she slept every night.

# CHAPTER FOUR

"I have something to tell you," Maggie said. She was seated on the bed in her room at the Dogwood House

"What's going on?" Ruby asked. "I know there's something happening. Brooks stopped by here and was pretty grim faced."

"The construction crew found something in the basement," Maggie said.

"Like a broken pipe?" Ruby asked.

"Like a human body," Maggie said. "The foreman realized there was a new wall in the basement in front of the regular one, so he started pulling the wall down and discovered some bones."

"Do you know who they belong to?" Ruby asked.

"I have no idea," Maggie admitted. "From what

I've been told, the bones have been there for a really long time."

"Do they think it was a murder?"

"It's looking that way," Maggie said. "It seems like the second wall was built to cover up the bones."

"Oh, my gosh," Ruby said. "Are you alright? Do you need somewhere to stay? I have room at the farm."

"Thank you, but I've already checked in at the Dogwood House. I want to be close to town in case something else comes up with the house."

"Okay, that's understandable," Ruby said. "I just can't wrap my mind around this. Someone has been dead inside in your basement all this time?"

"Yeah," Maggie said. "It's a lot to take in."

"Why don't you take off a few more days?" Ruby suggested. "We can handle things at work."

"No way," Maggie said bluntly. "I need to stay busy. In fact, before all of this exploded, I was at the Hunter Springs location whipping up a new donut with the guys. I actually have a fresh tray of them on the front seat of my car. I don't know how good they'll be, but I have them."

"Are you sure? We can add a new flavor to the menu any time," Ruby said.

"I'm positive," Maggie said. "I want to come in a little early tomorrow to make a batch."

"Do you have a recipe?"

"I do," Maggie said.

"If you send it to me, I can go pick up the ingredients after work," Ruby suggested.

"I can pick up the ingredients," Maggie said.

"Okay, but I was thinking that if you text me the list, I can pick everything up on my way home from the donut shop and we can make them at my house tonight," Ruby said. "Unless you have other plans."

"I don't know of any plans tonight," Maggie said. "Unless Brett needs me for something."

"If Brett needs you, he can come to my house as well," Ruby said. "I think you need a distraction."

"I do need a distraction," Maggie said. "I'll text everything over to you."

"Awesome. Be at my house at four," Ruby instructed. "In the meantime, call your son and let him know what's going on and where you're going to be. He will be worried about you."

"I hadn't even thought about letting Bradley know. I can't seem to think straight at all, honestly."

"He called me after you left the donut shop in Hunter Springs," Ruby said. "He wanted to let me know that you had some issues at the house and asked if I would check on you after work."

Maggie smiled slightly. "I have a good son," she said.

"You sure do. See you in a little while," Ruby said, ending the call.

She fished her charger out of her purse and plugged it in. She began to unpack her bags and hung a few things up in the closet in her room. When she finished, she decided to find Gretchen and fill her in on what was going in. Better to hear it from her than Orson.

Maggie slowly opened the door to her room and walked out into the familiar hallway. She was immediately visited by memories from her past years at the sprawling house, when her aunt would cook massive meals in the large kitchen while she read one mystery novel after another on the wrap-around porch.

As she walked down the steps, Maggie thought back in time. She knew the cottage house had belonged to her aunt in the early years. Marjorie had hung onto the property even after her husband built the larger house. The estate house, now a functioning bed and breakfast known as the Dogwood House, was a gift to her aunt for their later years. Maggie had fond memories of both places. She barely remembered her own home where she had lived with her parents. It never crossed her mind to drive by and look at the window that had once been her own bedroom.

A handful of renters had lived in the cottage over the years, but Maggie wasn't sure exactly how many. She did know that a few of the renters had lived in the house for multiple years at a time, and now it seemed as if there had been a murderer among them.

"How are you settling in?" Gretchen called to her from the kitchen. "Do you find your accommodations sufficient?" She laughed at her own joke.

"It's wonderful what you have done here," Maggie told her, as she had many times before.

"Are you going to be around for dinner?" Gretchen asked. "If you'd like, I can have Albert pick up some special food for you." Albert was Gretchen's all around handyman. "Either that or I can have Orson bring over some of your favorite things when he stops by later."

"Thank you, but I'm heading over to Ruby's farm to try out a new donut recipe," Maggie said.

"Oh, a new variety! I'm sure excited to hear that," Gretchen said. "Can you give me a hint?"

"Sure." Maggie nodded. "It's a coffee cream

brioche, and it's delicious. I made a batch with my son at the Hunter Springs donut shop earlier today."

"Oh, that does sound good," Gretchen said. "Any word on the house? Have they made any headway to fix the problem?"

Maggie took a seat at the kitchen island and rested her elbows on the counter. "I got a call when I was at the donut shop with my son. The foreman told me that I needed to come back right away, and that Brett needed to come with me. Imagine my surprise when I arrived and saw Brett already there."

"What was going on?" Gretchen asked her.

Maggie hung her head for a moment before looking up into the kind and concerned eyes of her friend. "You're going to hear about this soon enough, so I'll tell you everything I know so far," she said. "While they were checking on the fitness of the basement to bear a little more weight for the addition, Jimmy, the foreman, noticed an irregularity in the basement wall. He started looking around and it became clear that there was an extra wall added in front of the original wall."

"Oh, for a minute there, I thought you were going to tell me they found a secret room with a body inside." Gretchen clutched the front of her shirt and shook her head slowly.

"There wasn't a secret room, but they did find a body," Maggie said softly. "Well, bones."

"You're kidding, right?" Gretchen immediately dropped her hand from her shirt and frowned. "I mean it. You aren't serious."

"I wish I was kidding," Maggie said. "They found bones from a hand at first, but then they went a little deeper and found more. I left the coroner and her team there earlier with Brett, Brooks, and a handful of their coworkers."

"Holy crow," Gretchen said. She reached her hand across the table and covered Maggie's with her own. "They aren't suspicious of you, are they?"

"No, thankfully," Maggie said. "They said whoever it was, has been there for years. Many years."

"That's good," Gretchen breathed out the words. "I don't mean to say I'm glad someone was put in there, just that there is no suspicion on you."

"I have to admit that I feel the same way," Maggie said. "So, you can see the need for me to come here for a few days. I had offers from Ruby and from Brett, but I wanted to be closer to work, and to the house if something else comes up."

"Well, let's hope nothing more does," Gretchen said.

Maggie agreed and headed back to her room. She suddenly felt very tired and in need of a nap. What she really needed, though, was the chance to stop thinking for a little while. Because the truth was, her mind was starting to swirl around the thought that there might be something in her aunt's past that she didn't want to consider. As far as she had known, there had never been anything suspect in her Aunt Marjorie's life, but she hadn't known everything about her aunt's life, and now there was evidence that there were some deeply buried secrets.

# CHAPTER FIVE

"You know this entire thing may have absolutely nothing to do with you or your aunt," Ruby said while Maggie mixed vanilla paste into the cream cheese and heavy cream mixture. She followed it with the lemon juice and whipped it until it was evenly combined. She added the coffee granules and set the mixture in Ruby's fridge while they worked together on the brioche donuts.

"You mean a body buried in the basement wall in the house I inherited from her might have nothing to do with my family?" Maggie said wryly.

"It might not," Ruby said. She cut the brioche dough in circles. "I'm just saying, there's no need to get worked up over what you don't know yet."

"I wonder how long it will take for them to identify the body?" Maggie mused.

"I imagine they'll start with looking at missing people and go from there," Ruby said as she covered the dough. Maggie stared at her for a moment. They both grabbed their cell phones at the same time and smiled.

"How far back should we look?" Maggie asked. "Jimmy said something about at least fifteen years."

"Okay," Ruby said. "Let's check out missing persons from twenty years ago and work our way through."

"That sounds like a plan," Maggie said. She opened the browser on her phone and took a seat at the table. They sat together in silence for several minutes.

Ruby rose to work on the donuts before she returned to her seat. "Do you need a pen and paper?" she asked Maggie.

"Yes, definitely," Maggie said without taking her eyes off of her phone screen. She continued to read through old newspaper articles, while Ruby rose once again and retrieved two pens and a notebook from her kitchen drawer. She tore off several pieces and handed them over to Maggie.

Ruby returned to her seat and cleared her throat.

"I'm going back twenty-five years," she announced. "I think that's overdoing it, but I want to be thorough."

Maggie looked up from her phone for the first time in several minutes. "That sounds reasonable to me," she said. She picked up the pen and began writing names down on the page.

They continued their research until the timer to check the donuts startled them. Ruby rose again and checked the temperature on the deep fryer. One by one she began placing the donuts in the hot oil. The countertop fryer was made for home use and could only accommodate a half-dozen pastries at once. Maggie set her phone down and readied a clean, paper towel-lined cookie sheet to receive the donuts when Ruby brought them out.

"So, did you come up with much?" Ruby asked while she began removing the first batch.

Maggie nodded. "Eight names," she said. "At least, eight that seem the most likely, not that I know what makes something likely."

"I have eleven," Ruby said. "I concentrated my search to a one hundred mile radius around the county."

Maggie nodded. "I went a hundred miles out as

well, but only around the town of Dogwood Mountain and not the whole county."

"We need to compare our lists," Ruby said. "We might be able to eliminate certain names based on how long ago they went missing."

"Right," Maggie said. "And maybe we'll hear soon about whether we are looking at a male or a female corpse." She shivered suddenly.

Ruby sighed and held her metal tongs over the edge of the deep fryer. "Be honest with me, is this too much for you? If it feels too morbid, we can concentrate our efforts on other types of distraction."

"We're talking about a set of bones under my house, so of course, it's morbid but it's also helping. I can't stop thinking about how long I've lived there, not knowing there was a dead body buried just feet from where I take a shower every day."

"It's pretty weird to think about it that way, but if you feel comfortable about moving forward, I say let's compare notes and see what we come up with." She lowered the last of the brioche donuts into the oil.

Maggie set her tray on the kitchen island and retrieved the sweet cream filling from the fridge. She worked for several minutes to fill the extra-large injector Ruby had found among her barbecue tools.

One at a time, she filled the pastries with the coffee-flavored cream.

Ruby pulled a clean platter out of one of her cabinets and poured two cups of powdered sugar in the center. One at a time, she rolled each of the slightly cooled, filled donuts in the sugar and set them aside.

"These look so good," she said to Maggie when she had worked through the first tray.

"If we did it right, they'll taste even better than they look." Maggie arranged the last filled donuts on the tray and began the process of cleaning up while Ruby finished dusting them with the fine sugar. Twenty minutes later, they returned to their seats at the table and put their handwritten notes together. After eliminating a few names, Maggie leaned back in her seat.

"What about this name which technically was not a missing person?" Ruby said, pointing to a name. "I think the authorities assumed he was missing, but there never was a missing person report filed that I could find."

"I'm not sure," Maggie said. She read over the list and sighed. "We have three women and five men left."

Ruby nodded her head and traced her pen over the paper. "I think we should go back and see if there were any difficult circumstances associated with each name."

"What do you mean?"

"I mean, maybe there was a bad divorce, a criminal investigation or a lawsuit against one of them," Ruby said. "I don't mean we ought to eliminate the names entirely from the list, but we should set those aside for now."

"You're looking for here one minute, gone the next types of missing persons?"

Ruby nodded. "Right," she said. "Let's start with the names of people who were here one day and then gone without any possible explanation."

# CHAPTER SIX

"I'm down to two women and three men," Maggie announced a while later. She picked up another coffee cream brioche and took a bite.

Ruby swallowed the bite she had just taken before she spoke. "These are really, really good, Maggie," she said. "And I'm down to the same list."

"Let me read off the names I have just to make sure we don't have an outlier," Maggie said. "For the women, I have Loretta Smith and Linda Swanson."

"Same here," Ruby confirmed. "And the men?"

"Darrin Brown, Timothy Lorenzo, and Alton Mayes," Maggie said. She stopped and put the end of the pen in her mouth.

"What is it?" Ruby asked.

Maggie shook her head. "That last name, Alton

Mayes," she said. "It sure rings a bell, like I've heard it somewhere else before."

"Any idea where?"

Maggie shook her head again. "No, but it just sounds so familiar," she said.

Ruby picked up her pen and drew a large circle around the name.

Maggie's phone rang then. "Oh, it's Brett," she announced. She stood up to answer the phone and walked toward the back of the room.

"Hi, honey," Brett said when she answered. "Are you still at Ruby's?"

"I am. We just finished a batch of new donuts for the menu."

"Okay if I stop by?" he asked. Maggie wondered if he had heard anything she had said about the donuts.

"Sure, you can stop by," Maggie said, glancing at Ruby for confirmation. Ruby nodded her head and winked.

"Tell him to bring his appetite," she called on her way out the door to preheat the grill.

"Ruby said to bring your appetite," Maggie repeated.

"Good." Brett chuckled. "If she's cooking, I'm up to eating. We've had some developments late this afternoon. I think tonight is going to be a pretty long night for me and Brooks."

"Tell him I'll feed him when he gets here," Ruby said. She walked to her refrigerator and began pulling out ingredients.

"Did you hear that? You're in luck," Maggie said. She deliberately ignored his news about the investigation.

"I'll be there in twenty minutes," Brett said. "I do have something to talk to you about, Maggie. Okay?"

"I know," she said. "That doesn't mean I want to think about it while I'm waiting for you to show up, though."

"Understood," Brett said. "See you in a bit."

Maggie moved to the sink to wash her hands in order to help Ruby prepare dinner. "Did you really plan to feed us tonight?" Maggie asked.

"I didn't not plan on it," Ruby said with a smile. "I mean, I thought it was a possibility, so I thawed out some steaks and made a big salad when I got home."

"Steaks and salad? That's not planning on company for dinner?"

"Be quiet and cut up some potatoes for the air fryer," Ruby said. "I do want some healthy home fries to go with it."

Maggie chuckled and began washing a couple of

pounds of red potatoes in the sink. She set them on the counter next to the sink and began quartering them with the peels on. After the potatoes were cut, she rinsed them off again and patted them dry. She turned to preheat the air fryer when a memory hit her.

"I think Alton Mayes lived here in Dogwood Mountain when I was a teenager," she said. "I don't remember anything else, but I do remember that my parents knew him. Maybe he was an insurance agent or something. I just remember hearing or seeing his name when I was young."

"Did you know he was a missing person?"

"No, not at all," Maggie said, getting the potatoes going.

"But we don't know whether or not the body in your basement was male or female," Ruby pointed out. "Your memory might be a simple coincidence."

"Yeah, I know," Maggie said. "But it's interesting to me that his name brings back snippets of information."

"Can you grab the salad?" Ruby asked.

Maggie reached inside the fridge for the large, glass bowl. Ruby had anticipated company for sure. She had layered romaine lettuce, fresh spinach, arugula, and red cabbage on the bottom then added grape tomatoes, sliced cucumbers, red onions, shaved carrots, and feta cheese on top. The salad was colorful and amazing.

She turned back to the air fryer when the signal announced that it was finished. She pulled out the basket and tossed the potatoes around and started it again.

"Brett's here," Ruby announced when she stepped back inside after checking the grill. "He's still in his work truck."

"That doesn't surprise me," Maggie said. "He told me on the phone that it was going to be a long night."

"Knock knock," Brett called out before he stepped inside Ruby's kitchen. "What are you grilling?"

"Steaks," Ruby said.

Brett turned Maggie. "You do know if we get divorced, Ruby gets custody of me."

Ruby laughed. "I am not adopting you," she said. "But I could feed you, you know, out of charity."

"Hey, I'm not too proud," he said.

Ruby rolled her eyes when she moved past him to head outside.

"Be right back," Ruby said, heading outside with the meat.

"How are you?" Brett asked Maggie when they were alone.

She inhaled deeply and wrapped her arms around

his neck. "I'm still a little freaked out," she said. "But I'm settled into a room at the Dogwood House for the time being. I'm not sure what has made me more worked up, the fact that I've been living with a dead body in my basement or how worried I am that the work on the house will never get done."

"We'll worry about the house renovations when this is all over and done with," Brett said. "If the work on the house gets pushed back even a month or two, we will work things out."

Maggie pushed back from him. "Do you really think that this might take that long?" she asked.

Brett shook his head. "I didn't say that. I just mean, on the outside chance it does take that long, you and I are still going to figure this out together."

Maggie smiled. "I know. I'm just stressed out about all of this. I wish we had more information about who's in the basement, and why he or she was there."

"He," Brett said. "Dr. Marsh said the body in the basement belongs to a male."

"How does she know? Maggie asked.

"Well, they were able to gather the rest of the remains," Brett said. "She was able to determine from the rest of his bones that he was male."

"Right," Maggie nodded her head. "I should have known that."

"Should have known what?" Ruby asked when she returned from outside. She set the steaks on the counter and began removing plates from the cabinet.

"I should have known that the coroner could identify the gender of the body by looking at the rest of the skeleton," Maggie said.

Ruby looked up from the table at Brett. "Did they identify the bones?"

"No, but we do know that the body belonged to a man," Brett said.

"Did you tell him?" Ruby asked Maggie next. "About Alton Mayes?"

"Who is Alton Mayes?" Brett asked. He carried the platter of air fried home fries from the counter to the table and sat down. Maggie followed with the salad.

"We spent some time looking up missing persons from the area," Maggie explained. "Within a one hundred mile radius from here. And we came up with a name that I remember from somewhere."

"And that name was Alton Mayes?"

"Does it ring a bell to you at all?" Ruby asked. "Maggie was thinking it might have been the name of an insurance agent or something in town when you guys were kids."

Brett shook his head. "I don't recognize it," he said. "But you do? Are you sure?"

Maggie nodded. "I can't tell you where or how, but I have heard that name before," she said.

"We looked him up," Ruby continued to explain. "And we found that he disappeared about seventeen years ago."

"What other names did you come up with?" Brett asked. Ruby stood up and retrieved their notes from the counter.

"We looked these up independently and narrowed it down to these," she said and pointed out the final five they had written down. "Timothy Lorenzo and Darrin Brown were the names of the other men."

Brett folded the note over and tucked it in his pocket. "My staff is on this, too, but I will take this back with me," he said. "Might make my night go a little faster."

"These might, as well," Ruby said. She pulled a tray of the coffee cream brioche from the oven and set two in front of Brett.

"What is this?" Brett asked. He picked one of the donuts up and turned it over in his hand. "And can I have one before dinner?"

"Coffee cream brioche," Ruby smiled. "It is one of your fiancé's creations. And yes, dessert first, always."

Brett took a large bite and smiled. "You know, you guys do this to me every few months," he said. "You concoct some crazy delicious new donut variety, and you throw one at me, and it isn't fair. I have to maintain a certain level of physical fitness for my job."

"So, do you like the donut or not?" Ruby asked.

Brett chuckled. "This has to be one of my favorites. I love the soft pastry and the incredible coffee taste. This is so creamy, too."

"Okay," Maggie said. "I think that means this one is a success."

Brett left shortly after their real dessert. Soon after, Maggie helped clean up and drove herself back to the Dogwood House. She waved to Gretchen when she walked inside the house. It was just before eight when she took a quick shower in the bathroom attached to her room and settled into bed.

She tossed and turned for a solid hour before she got back up out of bed and searched her luggage for something to help her sleep. She found a bottle of a natural sleep aid and downed a tablet. She wrapped her robe around her and walked to the window, gazing outside at the familiar grounds below.

Gretchen and her handyman Albert had done an excellent job of preserving the landscaping in the yard. Maggie could gaze upon the entire estate and see the same care and quality her aunt had insisted upon when the house was still hers.

She turned away from the window and hugged her arms around her middle. Her memories did nothing to remind her, but she had to wonder if the same care had gone into her home, the cottage house, while it was a rental. And if her aunt had been as meticulous in the care of the cottage, how had the addition of a fake basement wall escaped her notice?

# CHAPTER SEVEN

The donut shop buzzed with activity the following morning. Maggie was grateful to return to her regular routine. She woke twenty minutes earlier than normal, dressed quickly, and let herself out of the bed and breakfast with as little noise as possible.

Ruby's truck was parked behind the donut shop when she arrived. "You're here early," Maggie said when she came into the kitchen.

"I wanted to get here and prep the new donuts. I'm also trying something different for the boxed lunches today. I had the idea after dinner last night."

"What is it?" Maggie asked.

"Flank steak salad with red onion, avocado, and fresh sweet corn." Ruby beamed as she worked. Maggie smelled the rarely used grill going for the first time. "I topped the salad with a creamy basil dressing. It's quite amazing if I do say so myself."

"Look at us, a new boxed lunch and a coffee cream brioche at the same time," she said.

"What in the world will our customers think?"

"There's a lot they might think," Orson said. He pushed the swinging kitchen door open and sauntered into the kitchen. "I've already been hearing some speculation from them about this. So, what is it that you want me to tell them when they bring it up?"

"You mean the flank steak salad or the brioche?" Maggie asked him, confused.

"No, no," Orson said. He shook his head and stared at her. "I mean about the discovery in the basement of your house. What do you want me to tell folks when they start asking questions?"

"Orson," Ruby said softly. "This might not be the right time to ask this."

"Then you tell me what I'm supposed to say to them when they ask me if there is a body buried in this building, too," he snapped.

"You can tell them that the minute I have any answers, they will have answers," Maggie said. Tears welled up in her eyes. She was frustrated and annoyed at her own weak response. "You tell them to watch the newspapers because they might actually know a little more about it than I do right now, and after that, you can ask them how it would feel to live in a house not knowing that something like that was just one level below where they laid their heads down to go to sleep each night. You go on and you ask them how they think this feels?" She pushed past Orson and went toward her office.

"Maggie," Orson said behind her. "Are you okay?"

"No," Maggie said flatly. "I am not okay. My house is in shambles. Some poor, unfortunate soul was buried downstairs and now there are people wandering around asking questions because they want to hear the latest gossip."

"I'm sorry," Orson said. "You have to know that I was only telling you the questions I've been asked. I really wasn't trying to cause you any distress."

"Oh, Orson," Maggie said. She dropped her shoulders and hung her head. "It's just because there's a lot going on in my head right now. I'm rattled. I guess that's the best way to put it."

"Rattled, huh?"

"I have no idea what's going on with my house. I have no clue if I'm going to find out that the victim is somehow linked to my family and what that would mean if he is. But mostly, I don't understand why there was a dead man in my basement in the first place. He has to have a family somewhere. What are they going to think? Were they still holding out hope that he was alive somewhere?" She felt the tears spilling down her face.

Orson took three big steps across the floor and stopped in front of her, wrapping his long arms around her. Maggie allowed herself to be hugged. She rested her head against his chest and wept. Orson said nothing more but held on for several moments. Maggie closed her eyes and allowed the stress to move through her. She could smell the cologne Orson wore mixed with vanilla.

"Do you feel better?" he asked when she finally pushed away.

Maggie shook her head and wiped her eyes. "I'm sorry," she said. "I know you were only trying to prepare me for what's been said."

"I was," Orson said. "But I could have been more sensitive about it. And you know that your family had nothing to do with some guy's death, right? I knew Marjorie Getz. I started coming into this donut shop the same day she opened it."

Maggie sighed and looked up at him. "Do you remember any of the people who rented my house from her back then? I was looking over the names of people who have come up missing around here in the past couple of decades."

"Did you come up with anything?" Orson asked.

"We came up with some names, but there was one we found that rings a bell to me," Maggie said. "I'm trying to think where I heard the name before. Do you remember a man named Alton Mayes?"

Orson's face fell. He stared at Maggie. "Where did you hear that name?" he asked.

"I just told you. Ruby and I just looked up the names of people who have been reported missing around this area going back twenty plus years," she said. "And this name, I don't know. I know it from somewhere."

"You need to leave this up to the police to figure out," he said. "Drop this." He walked away from her without another word.

Maggie followed closely behind him. "Orson," she said. He continued to walk through the kitchen without turning around to face her.

"What is going on?" Ruby asked her.

"Orson reacted oddly when I mentioned Alton Mayes," Maggie said. She stopped following him and watched as he headed straight into the employee restroom.

"Does he know him?" Ruby asked.

"I don't know for sure," Maggie said. "He just asked me where I heard the name and told me to drop it and let the police do their jobs."

"That's weird."

"Yeah, especially since right before that he was acting all fatherly and hugging me," Maggie said. "But as soon as I said something about Alton Mayes, he shut down and totally changed."

"I think we ought to leave it alone for now," Ruby suggested. "Let's get the day started and get these new brioches made. We can regroup this afternoon about Alton."

"Okay." Maggie headed for the cooler and began to collect the ingredients she needed for the cinnamon rolls she would start the morning's baking with. For the next several hours, she hardly looked up from the table while she mixed and then rolled out the dozens of cinnamon rolls that were a staple for the display case.

Orson made his way back through the kitchen several times. Maggie was unaware if he was looking at her when he passed, but she had the sense that someone was staring at her. Perhaps that had something to do with the mystery uncovered in her basement.

Myra and Naomi arrived at work somewhat

subdued. Myra made her way back to the baker's table and rested her hand on Maggie's shoulder. "Sorry about everything you're dealing with," she said.

Naomi made her way back to Maggie's side as well. She deposited a latte on the table in front of her and nudged her quietly with her shoulder. "Hang in there," she said.

Half an hour later, Myra returned and stood close to Maggie once more. "Brooks and Brett are out front," she whispered. "They want to talk to you."

"Right now?" Maggie asked. Her hands were covered in flour.

"I'll take over for you here," Myra said and handed her a towel. Maggie wiped her hands off and headed to the front. She exchanged looks with Ruby and pushed through the swinging door, looking around the packed dining room for the two men. She spotted them just outside the front door and wished she had brought her coat with her.

"What's going on?" she asked. "Do you want to talk inside?"

"No, we thought it might be better to chat out here," Brooks said.

"As you probably guessed, this is about the body

in the basement," Brett said. He removed his coat and hung it around Maggie's shoulders.

"I thought it might be," Maggie said. "What have you found out?"

"We have a preliminary identification," Brooks said. "And we have a bit of good news, too. After removing the body, we are positive that there is no one else down there."

Maggie stared at him wide-eyed. "I hadn't even considered that there might be," she said.

"Dr. Marsh has a preliminary match to Alton Mayes, the name you recalled," Brett told her.

"Do you know anything else about him?" Maggie asked suddenly. "Like do you know who he was or how he might be connected to my house?"

"We're working on that right now," Brett said. "We do know that he disappeared seventeen years ago."

"Was he married? Did he have children?" Maggie asked. The questions tumbled out of her mouth as fast as she could think of them.

"We don't have that information yet," Brooks continued. "But I do have the feeling that he wasn't married. His former business partner is the one who actually filed a missing person's report."

"What sort of business was he in?" Maggie asked.

Surely she would find some detail that explained her connection to his name.

"We're not exactly sure," Brett said. "He appeared to have been an investor in multiple businesses. He used to own part of the bowling alley downtown, a laundromat, and a couple of convenience stores in Hunter Springs."

"Who was his business partner?" Maggie asked.

"He was named Kevin Morgan," Brooks answered. "He died five years ago."

"We wanted to stop by and fill you in on what we know so far," Brett added. "However, you should know that information about this case is not going to be very easy to come by. This case is so old, and the clues so far are so sparse, we may not come up with very much."

Maggie nodded her head to indicate her understanding. "Have they, you know, finished with the basement? I mean, is the wall gone now?" she asked carefully.

"We are finished with the crime scene in the basement."

"I spoke to Jimmy just before we came here," Brett said. "So, I'm sure he will probably be calling you soon. He did tell me that they are assessing where things stand right now and will form a plan to move forward so long as you still want to."

"I think I want to," Maggie said. "I mean, do I want to?"

"I think we can take some time to think about what's best, but if you want to stay in that house, I'm all for it," Brett said.

"Will you go back to the Dogwood House right after work?" Brooks asked.

"That's what I'm planning to do," Maggie said. "I have to go and get a shower before I do anything else."

She had a lot of thinking to do. Until then, she had just wanted her house back, and now that it was close to happening, she wasn't so sure how she felt about it.

# CHAPTER EIGHT

Maggie drove back to the Dogwood House and rushed inside. She was glad that she was able to make it up the steps to her room without running into anyone on the way. She headed straight for the bathroom and took the hottest shower she could stand. When she finished, she stood in front of the mirror to dry off and dress quickly.

Back in her room, Maggie finally gave into her exhaustion and took a seat on the side of the bed. She sighed and ran her fingers through her still-damp hair. She ought to feel relieved that the extraction of the body in her basement was over. The police had left her property and her construction crew had resumed work, or at least embarked on assessing the damage and formulating a plan to move forward.

Shortly after Brett and Brooks left the donut shop after delivering the news, Jimmy had called her and repeated the same thing Brett had told her. He reassured her that they would have a plan in place by morning, and a day she could expect to return home if she was ready.

For some reason, relief was not what she felt at that moment. Her body was exhausted. She laid back on the bed and closed her eyes. A short nap might do her some good, but rest did not come. Instead, her eyes popped open, and she stared at the ceiling for several minutes.

Maggie sat up and swung her feet over the side of the bed when her phone rang. She didn't immediately recognize the number but answered anyway.

"Hello," she said.

"Maggie Sharpe? Dana Marsh, here. Dr. Dana Marsh. We met before."

"Yes, Dr. Marsh," Maggie said. "What can I do for you?"

"First, I apologize for calling you directly, but the sheriff has reassured me that you are not a suspect in the investigation into the corpse that was found under your home," Dr. Marsh said. "Anyway, I wanted to let you know that following a preliminary autopsy, I have determined the identification of the body to be that of

Alton Mayes. I know the sheriff had told you that was a possibility."

"He did," Maggie said. "But he said it wasn't confirmed."

"Well, it is now. We compared dental records, and we are listing him as the name of the victim," Dr. Marsh continued. "The other part of this is the fact that we also have determined a cause of death. I wanted to call you so you could hear it directly from me."

"Okay," Maggie said, wishing the woman would simply tell her what happened.

"The man was shot at close range," Dr. Marsh said. "I believe that he likely did not know what hit him, since the bullet entered through the back of his head."

"Oh, wow," Maggie said with a shiver. She hoped he didn't know what had hit him, or who had done it.

"How do you know he wasn't, you know, on his knees or something? Like in the movies."

"We are sure because we could tell if his head was bowed or in an unnatural position when he was hit," Dr. Marsh explained. "I know that sounds gruesome, but we have to understand everything in order to provide the police with the best information we can."

"Was there anything else?"

"Yes, but it is more of a technical nature," Dr. Marsh said. "We are quite sure that, based on the physical evidence from the body, he wasn't killed at your house. We think he was killed at another location and brought there."

Maggie exhaled slowly. "That's good to know, I suppose," she said. "Thank you for calling me to tell me, Dr. Marsh."

"Like when we met the first time, please call me Dana," Dr. Marsh said. "I'm hopeful that this information provides you with some closure."

Maggie sat up a little straighter. "Was there a relative or any other next of kin that has been informed of his death?" she asked. "Or at least, the circumstances of his death?"

"As a matter of fact, we were able to track down a sister living in Hunter Springs," Dr. Marsh said. "I can't give you any more information than that, but his family has been informed."

"Was it just his sister? I'm pretty sure he wasn't married with children, but did he have nieces and nephews? Anyone else?" Maggie asked. She wasn't sure why she wanted to know so badly, but she certainly did want to know.

"I'm sorry, I can't give you a lot of specific information," the doctor said. "As far as I can tell, the sister never married."

"Okay," Maggie said. She smiled into the phone. "I appreciate you calling me. Thank you, Dana." She ended the phone call and laid backward on the bed.

Alton Mayes had been shot. He was shot somewhere other than her house and brought there to be buried. Two things came as a relief to her. One, she was grateful to know that he had not been shot in her living room or while sleeping in the bedroom or anywhere else in her house, including the basement. The other thing she was grateful for was the idea that he might not have been aware of what was coming when he took his last breath. That gave her an odd sort of comfort.

Maggie closed her eyes for a second time. She rested for a good twenty minutes before a knock on her door brought her to her feet.

"Maggie, hon," Gretchen said on the other side of the door. "I brought you some tea."

She stood up and walked to the door, pulling it open to Gretchen smiling on the other side and holding a wooden tray.

"You didn't have to bring me tea." Maggie stepped out of the way so Gretchen could place the tray on the small table against the wall.

Gretchen began pouring hot water into the first small tea cup. "I thought you might like some refreshment after your workday," she said. She moved a cloth napkin off a plate and revealed two croissants. "I thought you could use a snack, too."

To Maggie's surprise, Gretchen poured water into the other cup. She pulled out a chair from the other side of the table and took a seat. Maggie pulled out the opposite chair and sat down. "You didn't have to do this," she said politely. "But thank you." She was still not sure how much she wanted company at the moment, but the thought was lovely. She waited while Gretchen spread homemade jam over one of them.

"I'll tell you, one of the strangest things I came across when I moved to this little town was the rumor mill and how fast word gets around about things," she said.

"It was the same way when I was in high school," Maggie said. She stirred half a teaspoon of sugar into her tea. "I never really knew how rampant it was among the adults until I moved back here."

"You spent a lot of time in this house when you were a girl," Gretchen said.

"I did," Maggie said.

"How does it feel to be here as a guest?"

Maggie set the croissant in her hand down and gazed at her friend. "I think it would feel different if there weren't so many questions floating around about the other house my aunt owned right now."

"I'm sure you do have a lot of questions," Gretchen said. She exhaled and looked out the window before she met Maggie's eyes again. "You know, there were some things left behind here."

"What things?" Maggie asked, full of curiosity.

"Albert found a filing cabinet in the basement," Gretchen said. "He was there looking for items to place in some of the rooms when we decided to redecorate a little bit last spring. I didn't mention it to you then because, quite honestly, it didn't cross my mind to do so until now."

"Why now?" Maggie asked. "Is there something there I need to see?"

"I'm not entirely sure, but I was curious when he found it and I looked through some of the drawers," Gretchen admitted. "All I found were some files and receipts, business papers, I think. You might find some of them interesting."

Maggie nodded. She understood at last what the older woman was driving at. "Is the cabinet still there?"

Gretchen smiled. "It is, actually," she said.

Maggie returned her smile. "Thank you for telling me about this," she said. "I think I might go exploring when we finish our tea."

"You would be welcome to do so."

# CHAPTER NINE

Maggie found the three-drawer filing cabinet just as Gretchen described it. She also found a curiously placed wooden chair under the window and took a seat. She pulled the unlocked middle filing drawer open and ran her finger along the tops of the file folder tabs. She pulled out one labeled "utility bills."

Inside the folder she found two years' worth of electric and water bills from the city of Dogwood Mountain.

She flipped through the invoices before she pushed the folder back into the drawer. She scanned the other labels and found phone bills, some dating back ten years or more. Other files included lists of events her aunt had hosted at the estate house.

After looking through the middle drawer, Maggie

stood up to explore the top drawer. She found more files with homeowners insurance bills, car insurance bills, medical and dental bills, and a variety of other expenses. She scanned a few folders and pushed them back in the tightly packed drawer.

She sighed and stood back. What exactly was she looking for anyway? So far, all she could find were personal details about her aunt and uncle's lives. Nothing tied them to Alton Mayes. She knelt down to the bottom drawer and pulled it out. Immediately, she took a seat and began pulling out several folders and piling them in her lap.

The first folder was labeled "donut shop utility bills." She flipped through the bills and smiled. Her own utility costs had surely gone up since her aunt opened the business.

She set the utility bills aside and opened the next folder labeled "employees." The file contained paper job applications and tax information. She smiled when she found Ruby's blank job application and other information. Unlike the others, Ruby's experience recommended her more than any job application could.

She scanned each name for a reference to Alton Mayes. Even a link to him through his old business partner would be something, she thought. Although she knew the police investigation would continue until the trail went cold, Brett had told her that it could take a very long time to find any information.

Maggie didn't want to wait that long to understand why a man had been murdered and then buried inside her house.

She reached toward the very back of the bottom drawer and prayed she would not find a nasty spider waiting for her. She pulled out three folders and shook off the dust and cobweb remnants that had accumulated on the top.

"Oh, wow," she said when she spotted the file marked "donut shop business plan." She opened the folder and smiled. The folder contained handwritten answers to a printed business plan from a template. Maggie scanned her aunt's answers. Most of her ideas were vague and far too general. She listed some of her goals as "bringing the community together" or "providing a place for senior citizens to gather to play bingo."

Early on, she had heard that her aunt's business acumen was not terribly sharp. In fact, she had heard from a few people that Ruby's help was what kept the donut shop afloat. Maggie closed the folder and shook her head. She chastised herself for even entertaining the idea that her aunt might have had anything to do with the murder of Alton Mayes. Her entire business plan was formulated around the idea of helping others.

Maggie flipped through the remaining folders and opened the last one. The file was unlabeled. She opened the manila folder and pulled out a bill of sale. Her eyes immediately went to the names of the sellers.

Alton Mayes, Kevin Morgan, and a third name, T.S Banner.

Maggie pulled the bill of sale from the file and set it to the side. She stacked the other folders back up and pushed them back into the drawer. She stood up with the bill of sale in her hands and brushed off the back of her pants. She pulled the chain on the light above her and headed straight for the stairs.

Maggie stopped by her bedroom and grabbed her phone and her purse before she headed to the kitchen.

"Did you find something?" Gretchen addled her.

"I found something. Something I need to get to Brett as soon as I can." She opened the back door and pushed on the storm door. Before she stepped out, she turned back to Gretchen. "Thank you for your help and for your friendship."

The older woman simply smiled at her and waved her off.

Maggie called Brett as soon as she got into her car. "I need to talk to you," she said when the voice-mail message beeped. Her phone rang less than a minute later.

"What's going on?" Brett asked her.

"Where are you?" she asked, not answering his question.

"At the coroner's office," Brett said. "Are you in danger?"

"No, no," Maggie said. She exhaled and dropped her shoulders. "I'm sorry if I sounded like that. It's just, I found something, and I think you need to see it."

"What is it? Does it have to do with the Alton Mayes case?" he asked her.

"Yes, actually," she said. "I was going through some things at the Dogwood House, and I found something with Alton Mayes name on it, along with Kevin Morgan's name and a third name I didn't recognize."

"What is it?" Brett asked.

"A bill of sale for the donut shop," Maggie said. "The building anyway. This shows that there was a link between my aunt and the man in the basement."

"Okay," Brett said. "Can you hang onto it for the time being? I am dealing with something here."

"What is going on?" Maggie asked.

"I can't say at the moment," Brett said. "It has to do with the investigation, and I am not at liberty to discuss it at this time."

"Okay," Maggie said. She was a little shocked at Brett's lack of interest in the bill of sale. "Should I drop this off at the sheriff's department in your office, then?"

"No, just hold onto it, Maggie," he said. "It isn't urgently important."

"But it shows that my aunt knew him," Maggie said.

"Yes, and that they had a legal business transaction," Brett said. "That doesn't prove anything, and the fact that Kevin Morgan's name is on it as well just shows what we already knew about their business relationship."

Maggie hung the phone up and pulled her car to the side of the road. She turned around and headed for the lake, where she could sit and think for a moment.

## CHAPTER TEN

Maggie held the bill of sale over her steering wheel and stared at the names listed on it for ten straight minutes. She read and reread the terms of the sale, the names of her aunt and uncle, and the address of the donut shop.

Nothing but the names on the bill stood out to her. Maybe Brett was right. What did a bill of sale tell her anyway? So what if her aunt and uncle purchased the building from the dead man? What did it prove?

Maggie set the document on the passenger seat. No matter how she tried to spin it to herself, she just couldn't get the thought out of her head. What sort of a coincidence was it that the body of a man her aunt and uncle had done business with had been hidden in a house they once owned?

Another thought crawled through her mind. Why on earth would her aunt leave a house to her with a dead man in the basement? A second after the thought entered her mind, Maggie decided that was all the proof she needed to prove that her aunt had nothing to do with Alton Mayes's murder. No way could she accept that her loving aunt would leave her a house that was also a tomb.

Maggie picked up the bill of sale again and read over the names of the sellers. She returned to the seller's line. T.S. Banner.

She reached for her phone again and quickly searched online for the name. "Thomas Banner, Farm Road 24, Dogwood Mountain, Missouri," Maggie read. She clicked on the map application and expanded the screen until she had a general idea where the house was at. Unfortunately, the remote rural location of the farm road did not give an exact location, not even the house number itself.

Maggie turned over the key in her ignition and backed her car out of her parking space. She checked her phone again for directions, then headed south. What she would say when she got there, she was less than sure. There was a good possibility that the address didn't belong to the person listed on the bill of sale.

The other possibility was that T.S. Banner, whoever they were, had died just like Kevin Morgan. Maggie wondered if she might find nothing but dead ends. No matter what she found, she was determined to put her own mind at rest.

Traffic was light through the county roads. She drove around the outskirts of Dogwood Mountain, close to the state line. The roads on the extreme southern side of the county were unfamiliar to her. She followed the map to the best of her ability but got turned around twice before she finally happened upon Farm Road 24.

Maggie turned onto the dirt road and drove slowly past the scattered mailboxes. Two miles down, she found what she was looking for. The mailbox was bright with red birds painted on the sides. The name "Banner" was stenciled in block letters across the top of the metal box. She took a deep breath and turned down the gravel drive.

At the end of the driveway, Maggie found a two-story farmhouse in bad need of a new paint job surrounded by an overgrown lawn. She hesitated in her car for a moment, unsure if the house was even occupied or if it had been abandoned. But after a closer look at the outside door, she spotted a small saucer filled with cat food and reasoned someone must be living there.

Maggie slowly opened her car door and stepped out. She listened for any signs of a watchdog before she went further. After a few seconds, she was sure the only outside animals she was going to run into were the half-dozen or so barn cats gathering around her legs.

She leaned down and patted a cat or two on their heads and then shut her car door. A small path led through the tall grass to the front door. Maggie exhaled slowly and knocked. She looked around behind her while she waited for a response. From where she stood, there was no sign of a car. She turned back to the door, seeing someone moving behind it. She stepped back and waited for the door to open. When nothing happened, she raised her hand to knock again. Before her hand connected with the door, it flew open. A white-haired woman in disheveled clothing stood frowning in front of her.

"Don't want your religion," the woman said and began to shut the door again.

"Wait, wait," Maggie said, putting her hand on the door. "I'm not selling religion or anything else."

"Then I guess you ain't got no business here," the woman said.

"That's not why I'm here," Maggie said quickly. "I'm looking for someone named T.S. Banner."

The old woman looked up at her for the first time. Maggie tried to read the look in her eyes, but the door slammed shut again before she had the chance.

"Ain't nobody here by that name," the woman said through the door.

Maggie closed her eyes. She tried to think. "I'm looking for the T.S. Banner who was in business with Alton Mayes and Kevin Morgan."

Maggie heard the movement behind the door suddenly stop. "Who's asking?"

"My name is Maggie Sharpe," she called back through the door.

"That name don't mean a thing to me."

"Maybe you knew my aunt," Maggie said fast. "Marjorie Getz. She owned the donut shop in town. She left it and a small cottage to me."

The door eased back open. The old woman stood in front of her. "Suppose you tell me what you want with me, then," she said.

"Are you T.S. Banner?" Maggie stood in the doorway staring at the figure in front of her. The old woman wore a loose fitting, faded cotton house dress. Her white hair stood up in shocks all over her head.

"Marjorie Getz really your kin?" the woman asked, avoiding the question.

Maggie nodded. "Yes, and I'm here because there was something found in my basement, and I am trying to figure everything out."

The old woman sighed. "Come on in," she said. "Wipe your feet."

Maggie complied and scooted her feet over the thread-bare rug in front of the door. "Thank you," she said.

"Have a seat and tell me what you want," the woman continued. "Make it fast."

Maggie took a deep breath. "I apologize for just showing up here," she began. "I came because I found a bill of sale for the building my business is located in when my aunt and uncle purchased it. I don't know if you've heard, but Alton Mayes's body was discovered in the basement of my house. I'm sorry if that is disturbing."

"Heard worse," the woman said. "Go on."

"Anyway, Kevin Morgan was another other name on the bill, and he passed away a few years ago," Maggie said.

"God rest his soul."

"Yes, of course," Maggie said. "The last name on the bill was T.S. Banner."

"So, you found Thomas Banner in the phone book and decided to look him up?" the woman asked.

"Actually, it was online," Maggie corrected. "We don't really have many phone books anymore. But, more or less, yes. I'm just looking to understand what happened."

"Apparently someone killed old Alton and stuffed him in your basement."

"Yes, clearly," Maggie said. "But what I want to know is…"

"Whodunit?"

Maggie nodded. "Mainly, I want to make sure that, well, none of my own were involved."

"Doubt that," the woman said. She turned toward the doorway and disappeared into another room.

Maggie remained seated on the old sofa where she had been directed. She could hear dishes clinking together in the other room. She had all but convinced herself to follow the old woman into the back of the house when she returned with a tray. She carried a pitcher of lemonade and two ice-filled glasses with her. "It ain't coffee, but the doctor says I can't have that stuff anymore."

"Oh, thank you," Maggie said when the woman handed over a glass.

"Connie Long," the woman said suddenly.

"I'm sorry?"

"My name," the woman said. "Connie Long."

"Nice to meet you," Maggie said. "I'm Maggie Sharpe."

"You already said that."

"I apologize," Maggie said. "I'm nervous."

"Why are you nervous," Connie asked her.

"I suppose it comes with the territory after learning about a dead man being buried in my basement," Maggie said.

"Point taken." Connie nodded. "You want to know if Thomas Banner is T.S. Banner, and if he was somehow involved in this man's death."

Maggie nodded her head. "I'm less interested in who killed him and more interested in knowing my aunt and uncle had no knowledge of it."

"Do you think your aunt and uncle had anything to do with it?" Connie asked her.

"No, I don't, but I also feel a little separated from what I should be thinking right now. I don't know if that makes any sense."

"Makes plenty of sense to me," Connie said. "You doing some remodeling? Is that how the body was found?"

"I'm getting married soon," Maggie said. "I wanted to expand the house a little bit. That's when my contractor found the false basement wall."

"And then he went to digging," Connie said. She threw her head back and laughed. Her laughter was followed by a coughing fit. "Sorry. That part hits my funny bone."

"I wish I could say the same," Maggie said.

"It will, when you go looking back at this," Connie said. She plopped into an armchair and pulled an oxygen hose to her nose.

"Are you okay?" Maggie asked.

"Emphysema," Connie announced. "It's what I get for smoking for fifty years."

"I'm sorry," Maggie said.

Connie shrugged. "Same thing took my parents and my older brother," she said. "Thomas Samuel was his name. Banner is my maiden name."

"T.S. is your brother, I take it?"

Connie nodded. She inhaled slowly. "Yes, and he was in business with Morgan and Mayes. If you're wondering whether or not he might have killed Alton, I wouldn't doubt it for a second. Thomas was as mean as any snake you ever met. And if we're talking a decade or so back, it probably was Thomas. He died two years ago sicker than a dog and weak as a kitten. So, if that body was brand new, I doubt it was him."

"They said it was probably fifteen years back or a little more," Maggie volunteered. She felt the tension in her shoulders begin to melt away. She wanted to stand up and run outside and declare to the world that her beloved aunt and uncle were not responsible after all.

Connie moved the oxygen cannula to the side and chuckled. "Probably was him then, to be honest," she said. "I can't tell you about one big falling out between Alton and my brother because there were probably several. Rumors were always going around about him burning down the house of one enemy or taking a wild shot at another. Now that you mention this, I kinda expect that new sheriff to come by at some point to ask me the same questions."

Maggie smiled. "He might, but I'll be sure to share the information you gave me with him as well."

"You know the sheriff that well, do you?" Connie asked. Her eyes narrowed as she spoke.

"He is who I'm marrying," Maggie's words must have hit the old lady's funny bone once again. She laughed until she coughed and slapped her knee as she did it. "Well, don't that beat it all," she said when she could speak at last. "My idiot brother murders his business partner and then buries him in basement of a house that one day will be owned by the wife of the county sheriff! That sounds just like something he would do."

"Do you really think your brother could be a killer?" Maggie asked, unsure if the woman was just cracking jokes or not.

Connie cleared her throat and leaned forward a little in her chair. "Yeah, I really do," she said. "Look, I know this isn't going to answer the questions you have or solve some mystery. Thomas is long gone, dead and buried. His secrets are buried with him, but he was an awful, terrible man. If his business partner was murdered, it's likely he had something to do with it. I'm sorry you got wrapped up in all of this."

"I'm sorry you had such a rotten human being for a brother," Maggie said. "I mean that."

Connie nodded. "He was real mean when we was kids. Shocked the heck out of me when he left me this house," she said. "Anyway, if you want to know more about Thomas, you ought to look up Donna Moore. She used to live east of town in an old trailer park."

"Who is Donna Moore?"

"Donna was the mother of one of Thomas's many children," Connie said.

Maggie left the older woman with a warm thank you and an invitation to come in for breakfast on the house the next time she was in town. She headed back down the long driveway and turned toward the highway. Before she reached the end of the road, she checked her phone for service.

"Good thing that went well," she mumbled to herself when she saw that she had no cellular signal whatsoever.

Connie had said that the woman had lived on the east side of town. Maggie was fairly sure she knew the trailer park so she turned in that direction, hopeful she would find a place along the way to pull over and find a proper address.

For November, the day had warmed up considerably. It was still cool, but the sun was shining high overhead. Maggie lowered her windows and let the air rush in. She smiled despite herself. The air felt terrific on her face and through her hair. She filled her lungs with it, then slowly exhaled. The tension and anxiety in her neck and shoulders eased.

Based on what the T.S. Banner's sister had to say, her aunt and uncle didn't have anything to do with the mysterious death of the man in her basement. His own sister believed him capable of murder. She even sent her in search of a woman who could verify his meanness.

It was the chime on Maggie's phone that alerted her to the fact that she had cell service again. She pulled over in the parking lot of a vacant flea market and after a fast search, she found an address for D.W. Moore. Maggie was sure the address matched up with the location of the trailer park. She stared at the screen and hesitated. The listing included a phone number. Should she call before just popping in? Showing up at Connie Long's house had been a gamble. Her luck might not hold if she showed up unannounced again, but she would never know until she tried.

# CHAPTER ELEVEN

Maggie slowed her car down when she pulled into the trailer park. She went down the first road and followed it through the center of the community. She found the single wide with the number eighty-seven painted on the side. The trailer was older but very well-kept. She was impressed with the two-level wooden deck built onto the front.

She parked her car on the side of the road, careful not to block the driveway. "Please let this go as well as last time," she said as she stepped out of her car.

The deck was as solid as it looked, somewhat out of character among the old and dilapidated homes. As she stepped up, Maggie noticed a built-in bench and flower planters. She smiled and approached the front door.

"Be there in a sec," a woman shouted when Maggie knocked on the front door. The door opened a few seconds later. "Can I help you?" The woman on the other side of the storm door was dressed simply in a pair of jeans and a sweatshirt. She was in her fifties, Maggie guessed. Her skin and face had a bit of youth left, but her eyes appeared dark and troubled.

"I'm looking for Donna Moore," Maggie said quickly.

"I'm Donna," the woman said wearily. "What can I do for you?"

Maggie exhaled before she spoke again. "This is going to sound weird, but I wanted to talk to you about Thomas Banner," she said.

"Nope, not today, not ever," Donna said and pushed the door shut.

Maggie thought fast. "The body of Alton Mayes was just found in my basement," she said. "I don't want or need anything, other than to find out if it is possible that Banner had something to do with it."

The door eased open again. "What good is it to bring up the dead?" Donna asked. Maggie noted the tears in her eyes. "Why come here bringing all of this up?"

"The truth is, I don't exactly know what I am bringing up," Maggie admitted. "My great-aunt was

Marjorie Getz. I just wanted to make sure that there was no way my family could be a part of it."

Donna sighed and pushed the screen door open. She moved to the side and let Maggie in. "Your aunt was not a part of it," she said. "If you are here to ask me if Thomas killed Alton, I can't tell you that for sure. I didn't see it and I don't have knowledge of it. If you're asking me if he could have done it, I would swear to it on the Bible."

"Really?" Maggie asked. "Connie Long told me that you had a child with him."

Donna nodded slowly. Tears began to flow down her face. She pointed to a series of photographs on the wall. "That's my son, James," she said.

Maggie stepped forward and gazed at the pictures of a young man. In one photo, he was holding a football. In another, he was smiling on the back of a motorcycle. "Looks like he grew up a good boy," she said, thinking of her own son.

Donna smiled and nodded her head. "He takes care of me," she said. "He's nothing at all like his father, at least who I think..." She trailed off and looked away from Maggie.

Maggie moved down the wall a little. The photos of the younger man aged some. She felt a lump forming in her throat. "Is there a chance that Thomas wasn't his dad?" she asked slowly.

Donna frowned again and hung her head. "It could have been Alton," she said quietly. "I hate to admit this, but I've only told a handful of people this. If he did kill Alton, that might be the reason why."

"What makes you say that?" Maggie asked. "Why do you think that might be the motive, Donna?"

"Because." Donna sobbed. "I told Thomas about Alton, and then Alton disappeared."

"Donna." Maggie stepped forward. "Is your son James, Jimmy, a contractor?"

Donna looked up at her and blinked. "How did you know that?"

"I think he is the foreman of the renovation on my house," Maggie said. "He's the one who discovered Alton's body."

# CHAPTER TWELVE

Maggie drove directly toward Dogwood Mountain. She thought about stopping to call Brett and tell him what she had found out. Instead, she drove straight for her own house. Her discussion with Donna was on her mind. She shivered to think that the young man who had been in her home for two weeks actually had an ulterior motive for being there.

As soon as she turned onto her road, she held her breath. The work trucks were still parked in front of the house, and Jimmy was there. Part of her really hoped Brett might happen to be there, too. She parked in front of the house and headed for the side where the work had been done. She found three of Jimmy's crew members standing outside and measuring the ground where the new crawlspace would be dug for the room addition.

"Where's your boss?" Maggie asked one of them when they turned around to look at her.

"Out back, talking to the sheriff," he said. Maggie sighed in relief when she walked around the house to find them.

"What's going on?" she asked when Brett looked up at her.

"I just had some questions for your contractor here," Brett said. His face was slightly drawn.

Maggie stopped and studied the two of them. "Something is going on between the two of you," Maggie said.

"I had an anonymous tip called into the sheriff's department this afternoon," Brett said.

"Let me guess," Maggie said. "They told you that someone was going around talking about Alton Mayes, am I right?"

"I think the phrase was *digging up old bones about the past*," Brett said. "Ironic."

"So, your boyfriend here thought it might be me," Jimmy said. He looked at Maggie and then looked away.

"Maybe it was Donna Moore," she said slowly. "Your mother."

"You spoke to my mother?" Jimmy asked.

"Why did you talk to Jimmy's mother?" Brett asked.

"Because I don't think it wasn't an accident that Jimmy took on this job," Maggie said.

"What are you talking about?" Brett demanded.

"Well, to start, I'm talking about this." She pulled the bill of sale out of her back pocket and handed it over to Brett. "This is from the sale of the donut shop to my aunt. The building, anyway."

"What am I looking for?"

"Here," Maggie said, pointing to the names of the sellers. "Alton Mayes and Kevin Morgan are listed, along with a third man, T. S. Banner." Brett studied the paper. "He was a very bad man." Maggie turned to Jimmy. "And you've been told your entire life that he was your father."

"Is that true, son?" Brett asked him.

Jimmy slowly nodded his head. "When I saw the advertisement for the job and the address, I knew it was the perfect chance to search for Alton."

"Why would you be looking for Alton?" Brett asked.

"Because you think Alton is your father," Maggie said. "At least, that's what you hope, isn't it?"

Jimmy hung his head. "Many years ago, he told

me that he had killed Alton Mayes," he said. "That's also around the time when he told me my mother cheated on him with Alton. He said that my father really was Alton Mayes and not him, but that if I ever told anyone, I would end up buried in a basement somewhere."

"And you've been looking around basements since," Brett said.

Jimmy nodded his head. "I couldn't do much of anything while he was still alive."

"And now you're on some sort of a mission, right?" Maggie said. "Or you were."

Jimmy nodded again. He looked up at Brett. "I swear to you that I am not a bad person, sir. I've never hurt another living soul and never plan to. I've just been hoping to prove that the man I was told was my dad, actually killed my father."

"Who were you trying to prove that to?" Brett asked.

"Mostly myself," Jimmy admitted. He turned to Maggie. "I'll have my guys continue doing the work after I clear out of here. You might want to ask Mike to head things up. He's the best I've got." He turned to leave.

"Wait a second," Maggie said.

"Maggie," Brett said quietly.

"I've got this," Maggie said. She turned to Jimmy. "You can't just pack up now. You have to finish my house, Mr. Moore. I'm trying to plan a wedding and I don't have the time to go looking for another contractor as good as you."

Jimmy turned around. "You mean, I still have a job here?"

Maggie nodded. "You better believe you do. I need this house in working order."

"Are you okay with this, Sheriff?" Jimmy asked.

Brett shrugged his shoulders. "My job here is to protect her. I don't think I have anything to worry about unless the wedding is delayed. That's when I have to start worrying." He smiled and clapped his hand on Jimmy's shoulder.

# CHAPTER THIRTEEN

"You knew," Maggie said when she saw Orson at work the next day.

"Knew what?" Orson asked her, not looking into her eyes.

"You knew who Alton Mayes was, didn't you?" Maggie asked.

Orson cleared his throat and threw the towel in his hand on the baker's table. "I knew the name, and I knew that his business partner rented your aunt's house for a short period of time. Beyond that, I only had suspicions," he said.

"Why didn't you share what you knew with me?" Maggie asked.

Orson sighed. "Because I didn't know the entire

story, and I didn't want to send you on one of your wild goose chases where you wind up in trouble."

"One of my wild goose chases?"

"Yeah, you know," Orson said. "Where you get one of those ideas in your head and wind up getting yourself in trouble."

"I don't think I like the direction of this conversation," Maggie said.

"And I don't like it when you run off and put yourself in danger," Orson snapped. "I don't like it one bit, Maggie. One of these days something is going to happen, and Brooks and Brett aren't going to be around to help you." He slammed his hand down on the table and walked off.

Maggie shook her head and headed in the opposite direction. "Sometimes I don't know what to think about that man," she said to Ruby when she returned to the front.

"Just think of him as the grumpy guy you hired to work in this place," Ruby said.

"You guys are forgetting something," Myra said. She swooped in from the dining room and stood behind the counter with them.

"What are we forgetting?" Maggie asked.

"You did more than just hire that grumpy old

man," Myra said. "You gave him a family and not just a job. He's assumed his role as protector."

"And he gets angry when he doesn't think we are doing enough to protect ourselves," Maggie said.

"Yeah," Myra said. "Exactly that. He just loves you, that's all."

"What are you going to do now?" Ruby asked.

Maggie sighed and shrugged her shoulders. "I guess I'm going to go find dear old dad and make things right." She found Orson standing in the cooler staring at the tubs of cream cheese on the shelf. "I remember the first day I met you," she said. "I was here running the donut shop by myself, and you demanded that I give you free donuts because that's what my aunt did."

Orson sighed loudly. "You didn't like me one bit," he said without turning around.

"Not at first," Maggie said. She chuckled. "And now look at us."

"Why did you let me stay on?" Orson asked. "I mean, after I was so demanding and all."

"I don't really know what it was at first," Maggie said. "But I know what it became."

"What is that?" Orson asked her.

"Family," Maggie said. "That's what it is now. And you know something else, Orson? I wonder what things would be like if you hadn't shown up here, demanding donuts like you did."

"Maybe a little bit calmer." Orson grinned.

Maggie shook her head. "I don't think so," she said. I think you started something for me. Forced it, maybe. You made me open my eyes and my heart and now look at the mess I'm in." She wrapped her arms around him and hugged him tightly. "I love you, too, you big old grump."

\*\*

**If you enjoyed Breakers Dozen, check out the next book in the series, Rolling in the Dough, today!**

## AUTHOR'S NOTE

I'd love to hear your thoughts on my books, the storylines, and anything else that you'd like to comment on—reader feedback is very important to me. My contact information, along with some other helpful links, is listed on the next page. If you'd like to be on my list of "folks to contact" with updates, release and sales notifications, etc.... just shoot me an email and let me know. Thanks for reading!

Also...

... if you're looking for more great reads, Summer Prescott Books publishes several popular series by outstanding Cozy Mystery authors.

## CONTACT SUMMER PRESCOTT
## BOOKS PUBLISHING

Blog     and     Book     Catalog:     http://
summerprescottbooks.com
   Email: summer.prescott.cozies@gmail.com

And…be sure to check out the Summer Prescott Cozy Mysteries fan page and Summer Prescott Books Publishing Page on Facebook – let's be friends!

To sign up for our fun and exciting newsletter, which will give you opportunities to win prizes and swag, enter contests, and be the first to know about New Releases, click here: http://summerprescottbooks.com

Made in United States
Orlando, FL
15 May 2023

33161281R00065